A catalogue record for this book is available from the British Library

Published by Ladybird Books Ltd
A subsidiary of the Penguin Group
A Pearson Company
LADYBIRD and the device of a Ladybird are trademarks of Ladybird Books Ltd Loughborough Leicestershire UK

© Disney MCMXCVII

Based on the book by Dodie Smith.
Published by William Heinemann Limited.

Disney's **101 DALMATIANS**

Ladybird

*B*rrinng! *Brrinng!* The alarm clock rang and rang, but Roger didn't stir. He was fast asleep, and it seemed that nothing could wake him.

Nothing, that is, except Pongo, his faithful Dalmatian. Pongo knew that Roger had an important appointment, and he wanted to get his master up in time. He leapt onto the bed and nudged Roger with his cold, wet nose.

"All right, all right," muttered Roger, stumbling out of bed at last. After a shower and a quick cup of coffee, Roger took out his bicycle, and he and Pongo set off.

Roger was a designer of video games. So far he hadn't had much success, but this morning he was showing his newest game to one of the biggest toy companies in the world. If they bought the game, his worries would be over.

At the toy company, an executive led Roger to a conference room and introduced him to a young boy.

"If he likes it, the game's a winner," the executive explained to Roger. "If he doesn't like it, we're not interested. He's never been wrong yet."

"If you have any suggestions, I can always make changes," Roger told the boy nervously.

But the boy ignored Roger. He watched the screen and moved the joystick without much enthusiasm.

"Good graphics," he said, when the game was over. Roger smiled hopefully. "But that villain's just too nice to be interesting. It'll never sell!"

"Sorry," said the executive to Roger.

Disappointed, Roger left the office. Pongo was waiting patiently for him just outside the building.

Not far away, at the headquarters of De Vil Fashions, a young designer named Anita was sketching a black-and-white-spotted outfit. Her boss, Cruella De Vil, looked on.

"Spots! I love it!" Cruella cried. Then she noticed a photograph of a Dalmatian on Anita's desk. "What a darling dog!" she gushed. "Is it yours?"

"Yes," said Anita quietly. "Her name is Perdy."

As Cruella looked at the photograph of Perdy, an evil idea formed in her mind. *Imagine if we made an outfit in* real *Dalmatian fur*, she thought. *It would be simply marvellous!*

Anita thought Cruella had acted most odd when she had seen Perdy's photograph. But she tried not to think about this when she left the office later. As she cycled through the busy streets of London, she was looking forward to an afternoon playing in the park with Perdy.

Perdy, on a lead attached to Anita's handlebars, ran along gracefully beside the bicycle. She was eager to get to the park, too.

As they travelled across the city, the pair passed Roger on his bicycle, with Pongo loping along beside him. The moment he saw Perdy, Pongo's heart leapt. He had never seen such a beautiful Dalmatian before. He had to catch up with her!

Instantly Pongo tore after Perdy, pulling an alarmed and bewildered Roger behind him.

"Pongo! What's got into you?" Roger spluttered as they moved wildly through the midday traffic. But Pongo just galloped faster, desperate not to lose sight of the beautiful female Dalmatian.

"Slow down! Stop!" Roger screamed. Car horns blared and passers-by crashed into one another as they tried to avoid the madly speeding pair.

As they zoomed into the park, Pongo tugged so hard at his lead that it snapped. As Pongo raced ahead, the bicycle hurtled out of control, crashing into a park bench and sending Roger flying headfirst into the lake.

At last Pongo reached the hillside where Perdy was playing with Anita. Joyfully Pongo sprinted back and forth, trying to get the lovely Dalmatian to notice him.

Meanwhile, a wet and bedraggled Roger managed to haul himself out of the lake. Looking around for Pongo, he saw a Dalmatian playing nearby. "There you are!" he muttered.

Quickly, Roger crept up behind Perdy and grabbed her collar. "Now I've got you!" he cried.

"What do you think you're doing?" shouted Anita, rushing over angrily. "You let my dog go this minute!"

"*Your* dog?" said Roger, confused.

A moment later, Pongo bounded up to Roger, wagging his tail enthusiastically.

Embarrassed, Roger apologised to Anita and explained what had happened. As he and Anita gazed at one another, they both realised something special was happening. At the same time, their Dalmatians were beginning to get acquainted.

Anita lived very close to the park, so she invited Roger to her flat to get dry. There, as the two sat and talked, their feelings for one another deepened. As Roger and Anita kissed in front of the crackling fire, Pongo and Perdy snuggled up as well, happy to be together.

A few months later, Roger and Anita stood facing one another at the altar of a large and beautiful old church. They couldn't have been happier. As they had spent more time together and got to know one another better, they knew for certain that they wanted to be together always. And so here they were, about to be married.

Their friends and loved ones surrounded them, the choir sang, and the page boy and bridesmaids gazed adoringly at the happy couple.

As the minister began to speak, Roger turned his head slightly to look up the long aisle of the church. He grinned, and with his eyes signalled to Anita to look as well.

Anita followed Roger's gaze up the aisle, and when she saw what he was looking at, she grinned too.

There were Pongo and Perdy, gazing lovingly at one another and looking as if they, too, were about to be married!

Roger and Anita exchanged their vows, and the minister concluded the ceremony. The bride and groom kissed – and Pongo and Perdy bowed their heads.

A moment later, the sound of church bells filled the air, and Roger and Anita joyfully made their way up the aisle. They were on their way to their new life together – along with their two happy Dalmatians!

Meanwhile, Cruella De Vil was still thinking about Anita's designs. She was now determined to create an outfit made of real Dalmatian fur.

Cruella loved fur – *real* fur, from *real* animals. And she would go to any lengths to get that fur. She knew she could always rely on the help of her two 'assistants' – a pair of crooks called Horace and Jasper. She rang them up and told them what she needed.

"I want some Dalmatians," she told them. "Preferably puppies, with nice, soft fur. And you're going to get them for me, do you understand?"

Later that day, Horace and Jasper came to see Cruella. They had something they were sure would please her – the skin of a rare white tiger they had stolen from London Zoo. An evil man called Mr Skinner had helped them with their terrible task.

Cruella was thrilled with the tiger skin. "Oh, you big, beautiful darling," she crooned, running her fingers through the silky fur. Wrapping the fur around herself, Cruella modelled it in front of one of her many mirrors.

"Black and white suits you," Horace said, trying to flatter her.

But that only reminded Cruella of what she really wanted now – Dalmatian skins. Angrily, she threw the tiger fur aside.

"Go back to your hovel and wait for orders!" she shouted at Horace and Jasper.

The days were passing happily for Roger and Anita, and for Pongo and Perdy. They had all moved into a cosy house near the park, and a kind woman called Nanny had come to be their housekeeper.

One morning, Anita noticed a change in Perdy. Over the next few days, she watched Perdy carefully, and soon she was sure she knew the reason for the change. All the signs were there.

"Perdy's going to be a mother!" she told Nanny and Roger happily.

Weeks passed, and at last it was time for the puppies to be born. On a rainy autumn afternoon, Perdy settled into the basket that Nanny and Anita had prepared for her. Roger and Pongo tried to stay calm as they waited in the living room.

Perdy lay in the cosy basket, which had been placed in a quiet corner of the kitchen, where she wouldn't be disturbed. Anita sat with her, waiting patiently. Every now and then Perdy whimpered a bit, and Anita stroked her comfortingly.

After some time, Perdy began to stir restlessly.

"Tell the boys it will be any time now," Anita said to Nanny.

Nanny went out to tell Roger and Pongo, who were pacing back and forth between the sofa and the kitchen door. Then she rushed back to help Anita and Perdy.

Roger and Pongo were still pacing anxiously when Nanny rushed back into the living room.

"They're here! The puppies are here!" she cried, excitedly. Then Nanny hurried back into the kitchen.

"There are five puppies," Nanny called. "No, there are six... seven... eight!" On and on it went, until Nanny finally announced, "*Fifteen* puppies!"

Roger was about to congratulate the proud father when Nanny came back into the living room. She was holding a small, still bundle of fur wrapped in a towel. "Only fourteen," she said sadly. "We lost one."

Roger took the tiny creature and showed it to Pongo, who licked it gently. After a moment, the little puppy began to stir.

"It's alive!" Roger cried happily. "We *do* have fifteen puppies! We'll call this one Lucky," he told Nanny.

Nanny took Lucky back to his mother. A few moments later she appeared at the door again. "You may go in now, Pongo," she said. Slowly and carefully, Pongo padded into the kitchen. He and Perdy exchanged a tender nuzzle, and then Perdy introduced him to their brand-new family.

Roger, Anita and Nanny were thrilled. They already adored Pongo and Perdy – now they had fifteen more precious Dalmatians to love and cherish!

The puppies grew quickly, and soon their cosy basket could barely hold them all. They were all playful and curious, and they were constantly discovering new ways to have fun – and to get into mischief!

Before long, the puppies began to develop their own individual personalities. Roger and Anita could see that each one was different, and special in its own way.

The one they called Fidget was the liveliest. Wizzer was the bravest. And Lucky – well, he was born lucky and stayed that way. No matter how much trouble he got himself into, he always found a way out!

One blustery evening, as lightning flashed and thunder boomed, Roger and Anita heard a knock on the door.

It was Cruella De Vil.

"Anita, darling!" she cried, pushing her way into the house. "I understand you have some Dalmatian puppies."

"That's right," said Anita. "In fact, we have fifteen."

"Fifteen puppies! How perfectly marvellous!" said Cruella, pulling out her cheque book. "I'll take them all."

Roger was furious. "I'm sorry, Cruella," he said, trying to control his anger. "The puppies are not for sale."

"Nonsense!" Cruella said. "You can't turn down an offer like this! Name your price – how much per spot?"

But Roger refused to change his mind.

"Fools!" screamed Cruella. "You'll be sorry for this!" She stormed out, slamming the door behind her.

Roger and Anita didn't hear from Cruella again, and soon they had forgotten all about her unpleasant visit.

One evening, Roger and Anita took Pongo and Perdy out for a walk in the park while Nanny stayed at home to look after the puppies.

Roger and Anita sat on a bench while Pongo and Perdy listened to dogs barking in the neighbouring streets. This was the 'Twilight Bark', which was used by dogs everywhere to report the latest news.

As Roger and Anita happily discussed their plans for the future, they had no idea that something terrible was happening at home. Cruella's evil 'assistants', Horace and Jasper, had been watching them. As soon as Roger and Anita had left, the two criminals had forced their way into the house and locked Nanny in a cupboard!

Ignoring Nanny's muffled screams, Horace and Jasper headed straight for the kitchen.

"You hold the bag," said Horace, handing Jasper a heavy sack. "I'll get the puppies."

The puppies whimpered with fear, but there was no way to escape. One by one Horace grabbed them and put them into the sack. Then they drove out to De Vil Manor, Cruella's dilapidated old mansion in the country.

Cruella was delighted when Horace rang to tell her that they had the puppies. "My faith in your limited intelligence is temporarily restored," she said. "I'll send Mr Skinner out there soon – to get the fur!"

Roger and Anita were horrified when they discovered what had happened. As soon as they had freed Nanny, they phoned the police, who immediately launched an investigation. Roger suspected Cruella, but the police could find no evidence against her.

Pongo and Perdy were heartbroken, and terribly worried about their puppies. They knew there was only one way to find out what had happened to the puppies – use the Twilight Bark.

The following evening, Pongo scampered up to the rooftop and barked out the news: "Fifteen Dalmatian puppies stolen."

Pongo's anxious message went out across the park, and from there to dogs in the surrounding streets. Before long it had reached dogs all over London, who in turn sent it far out into the countryside.

Late that night, the news found its way to a gentle sheepdog called Fogey, who lived on a farm not far from De Vil Manor.

Fogey hurried to the barn to tell the other animals what he had heard. A terrier called Kipper remembered that he had seen a van taking some puppies to De Vil Manor earlier that evening.

Together, the animals worked out a plan. While Fogey barked out a message to be carried back to Pongo and Perdy, Kipper raced off to the De Vil house to find out what had happened to the puppies.

Inside the crumbling old De Vil house, Horace and Jasper were waiting for Mr Skinner to come for the puppies. They sat on torn, shabby chairs by the fire, trying to stay awake.

"I don't like this job," Jasper complained. "And I don't like that horrible Mr Skinner. I wish we'd never got mixed up in all this."

"You won't say that tomorrow, when Cruella gives us all the money she promised us," Horace said. "Try to be patient. We just have to wait a few more hours, and it will all be over."

Meanwhile, Kipper had managed to sneak into the house through a crack in a wall. As he crept down a dark, musty corridor, he heard a faint cry. It sounded like a puppy!

Following the sound, Kipper found his way to the library. Sure enough, he found the puppies. But there weren't just fifteen of them – there were *ninety-nine* frightened Dalmatian puppies! Kipper couldn't believe his eyes.

Kipper knew he had to help the puppies escape before anything happened to them. Quickly and quietly, he began rounding them up so he could lead them out to safety.

Hearing strange noises, Horace and Jasper decided to see what was going on. They grabbed broken bits of furniture to use as weapons, and went out to the hallway.

The crooks were expecting to sneak up on an intruder, but they were so clumsy and bumbling that they ended up hitting each other on the head!

A moment later, they spotted the puppies in the hallway upstairs. "Get them!" Horace shouted.

As the two men charged after the puppies, the old staircase gave way. Horace and Jasper both crashed through the rotting wood.

Kipper kept a close watch on the puppies as they hurried through the house. He wanted to get them to the top floor, where he could lead them out through a window.

Meanwhile, Horace and Jasper were trying to free themselves from the mess they had got themselves into. Jasper groaned with pain.

"We have ninety-nine dogs to find," Horace shouted impatiently. "Stop complaining and let's get going!"

They finally reached the landing and were getting closer to the puppies. But brave little Wizzer managed to distract them. While the puppies went ahead with Kipper, Horace and Jasper ran after Wizzer – and fell right through a hole in the floor.

The puppies followed Kipper through endless dusty hallways and made their way through one cluttered, untidy room after another. The big, sprawling house seemed to go on for ever.

Kipper and the puppies all got a fright when one of the puppies slipped and bumped into a table. A big, heavy lamp fell over and smashed on the floor. Fortunately, no one was hurt.

Horace and Jasper, however, had heard the noise. Instantly, they came rushing to investigate. The puppies managed to get away just in time. But when Kipper counted the puppies, he discovered that one was missing. Where was Wizzer?

Once again, Wizzer had hung back to throw the criminals off the track. Running after him, Horace and Jasper headed back towards the staircase.

But before the bumbling pair had got very far, the stair carpet slipped, pulling down a large cupboard full of china. It crashed and clattered down the stairs and finally landed right on top of Horace and Jasper. Their groans of dismay were drowned out by the sound of shattering plates, cups and saucers.

It took a few minutes for the two clumsy crooks to come to their senses, and then they began to grope their way out of the confusion of drawers and bits of broken crockery. This gave Kipper and the puppies just enough time to make their way up one last rickety staircase to the open window on the top floor.

Under Kipper's watchful eye, the puppies filed out of the window and onto the roof. Then one by one they slid down a slippery drainpipe and landed in the snow.

Fogey, who was waiting for the puppies, guided them to a nearby field. They thought they were safe at last, until they heard a car approaching. It was Cruella De Vil!

Cruella rushed into the house, eager to see all the Dalmatian puppies. When Horace and Jasper told her the puppies had escaped, she flew into a rage.

"You dimwits!" she screamed. "Whatever it takes, catch those puppies!"

On the way back to her car, Cruella noticed some puppy tracks in the snow. She couldn't see any other sign of the puppies, but she decided to follow the tracks in her car.

Fortunately, the puppies were now safely hidden in the flock of sheep that Fogey looked after. Snuggled in amongst the warm, woolly coats, the puppies all held their breath as Cruella stopped her car and gazed out across the field. But all she could see were sheep, so she drove on.

Once Cruella was gone, Fogey barked out his orders to the puppies. Slowly they crawled out from under the sheep and followed Fogey across the cold, snowy field. He was taking them back to his farm, where he knew they would be safe – for a while, at least.

At last the puppies reached the farm. Fogey took them into the barn, where the cows gave the hungry puppies a long, welcome drink of fresh, warm milk.

Meanwhile, Pongo and Perdy had received Fogey's message and set out from London. Though they were exhausted from their long journey, they were happy and excited when they finally reached the farm. They could hardly wait to see their puppies again.

The animals in the barn greeted Perdy and Pongo warmly and directed them to the cows' stalls. The two dogs rushed ahead eagerly.

Pongo and Perdy greeted their puppies with joyful yelps and loving nuzzles. They were all thrilled to see one another.

But Pongo and Perdy weren't expecting to see eighty-four more Dalmatian pups!

There were happy, playful Dalmatian puppies everywhere! Pongo and Perdy looked around in amazement, wagging their tails excitedly. They had never seen so many puppies, and they were delighted. They knew, of course, that there was only one thing to do – they would have to take all the puppies home with them.

But amidst all their joy, the Dalmatians sensed danger. Sure enough, a moment later, Fogey barked a warning from outside the barn. Trouble was on its way!

Cruella De Vil's car had pulled up outside the barn. The Dalmatians heard the car door slam, followed by loud footsteps coming up the path.

"Come out, little puppy dogs," Cruella called, trying to make her voice sweet and gentle. But the Dalmatians weren't fooled. They stayed right where they were.

Cruella tried to peep through a hole in the barn doors, but all she could see was the back of a horse.

"Oh, little sweetie puppy dogs," Cruella called again, "it's time to come out now."

Suddenly the horse gave the barn doors a mighty kick. They flew open, throwing Cruella high into the air. As she landed, a group of squawking chickens pelted her with eggs.

While Cruella struggled to recover, the Dalmatians were streaming silently out of the barn. By the time Cruella realised what was happening, they were all gone.

"I'll get you!" Cruella screamed. "You can't escape from me!" She began to chase the puppies, but before she got very far she tripped and tumbled through a hole in the barn floor.

SPLAT! Cruella fell right into a vat of sticky, gooey molasses. By the time she managed to get herself out, she could barely move, much less run after the Dalmatians.

Meanwhile, the police had uncovered evidence against Cruella and her accomplices. After arresting Mr Skinner in London, they had sped out to De Vil Manor, where they picked up Horace and Jasper. They soon caught up with Cruella, who had to join the others in the police van.

"I'm ruined, and it's all your fault," she snarled at Horace and Jasper. "You were outsmarted by a pack of puppies!"

Horace and Jasper didn't argue with her. They were so relieved that the whole nasty business was over, they didn't even mind going to prison.

The puppies, led by Pongo and Perdy, trekked across the countryside to the nearest village – where they were met by a crowd of police officers. The police had been scouring the countryside for the fifteen missing puppies, and were amazed to see how many Dalmatians were coming towards them now!

It took the officers a long time to round up all the puppies, but at last all the puppies – as well as Pongo and Perdy – were safely inside the police cars.

"I counted ninety-eight puppies, plus the two parents," said a policeman to his sergeant. "That's one hundred Dalmatians altogether."

All at once Kipper came trotting up the road, accompanied by Wizzer. The policeman and the sergeant looked at one another. "Make that one hundred and *one* Dalmatians!" they said.

At long last the puppies were safe and on their way home.

"They're here! Hurry!" cried Nanny, when she saw a police car pulling up in front of the house. She came rushing out, followed by Roger and Anita.

Pongo, Perdy and their puppies leapt out of the car and into the welcoming arms of their owners. There were happy smiles and cuddles for everyone.

"Thank you, gentlemen," said Roger to the police officers. "We're so grateful for everything you've done."

All at once another police car rounded the corner. Then came another, and another… Roger and Anita exchanged puzzled glances as they watched the long line of police cars drive up to their house.

The doors of the police cars opened, and Roger and Anita watched in astonishment as eighty-four Dalmatian puppies bounded out onto the pavement.

"They were with your puppies," a policeman explained.

"What will you do with them all?" asked Anita.

"We don't really know yet," the policeman replied. "We were hoping that perhaps you could help us out…"

Roger and Anita looked at one another and smiled. Each knew what the other was thinking.

"The puppies can stay with us," said Roger.

At first Roger and Anita weren't sure how they would find room for one hundred and one Dalmatians, but somehow they managed.

Before long, all the puppies were happily settled in their new home. With Cruella De Vil and her evil gang safely locked up in prison, there was nothing to worry them. They romped and played together, and enjoyed being one enormous family.

But as the puppies grew, the house began to seem smaller. And then one day Anita had some happy news for Roger – they were going to have a baby of their own!

Roger, Anita and Nanny were thrilled, of course, but they knew they couldn't stay where they were.

"We'll have to find a bigger house," said Roger.

Fortunately, Roger had come up with a brilliant idea. Inspired by Cruella De Vil, he had created the perfect villain for his video game. This time the toy company – and their young advisor – loved the game, and it became a huge success.

With the money from the game, Roger and Anita bought a big house in the country – with lots of space for the puppies to play.

Roger and Anita now had the perfect place to raise their new family – and their one hundred and one Dalmatians!